Mail Order Misunderstanding

Book thirteen in the Brides of Beckham

Kirsten Osbourne

Chapter 1

JULIA RUBBED THE BACK of her neck tiredly. She was off for an adventure, and she was excited, but after being on a train for ten days, she was exhausted. She wanted nothing more than to curl up in bed for a week, but her first teaching assignment would begin on Monday, and it was already Friday. She needed to go to the schoolhouse and make certain everything was ready for school to start.

Julia had flame red hair and green eyes. She knew she wasn't a beauty, but small children didn't run screaming when they saw her coming either. She was tall with a slender build. Her dream, since she was a child was to be a schoolteacher, and finally, it was happening for her. In all her eighteen years, she'd never been so nervous and excited all at the same time.

When the train pulled into the station in Weatherford, Texas, she immediately looked for the stagecoach, which the letter she'd received had told her she would take. She had the ticket in her hand. She picked up her carpet bags and got off the train, walking straight to the stage. She handed the driver her ticket and climbed onto the stagecoach, glad to finally be off the bumpy train, but not looking forward to another four hours of travel on the stage.

Wiggieville, her destination, was four hours west of Fort Worth, and despite its strange name, it sounded like a quaint small town she would be pleased to call her home. She looked across at the companion on the other seat and smiled sweetly. "I'm Julia Simmons."

The older lady sitting there nodded regally. "I'm Mrs. Davis. I'm on my way to visit my grandchildren."

"Oh, where are you headed?" Julia asked. She knew very little about the area, except that Wiggieville needed a teacher, and she planned to be the best teacher ever seen in the small town.

"I'm going to Mineral Wells."

Julia shook her head. "I'm afraid I don't know much about Texas geography. I'm here from New York to teach at the school in Wiggieville." She spoke of her future profession proudly. She'd studied hard for years and had finally passed her tests to allow her to become a teacher just a month before.

Mrs. Davis smiled. "I'll go on for a bit longer than you will. Wiggieville is a nice place about an hour out of Weatherford. A friend of my son named it after his grandmother."

Julia frowned. "How could a place like Wiggieville be named after a person?" Who on earth would name someone 'Wiggie?'

"Well, all the children in his family called their grandmother 'Wiggie.' So when he founded a town, he named it after his grandmother, whom he loved dearly."

Julia shook her head. "Why did they call her Wiggie?" In New York, where she'd come from, grandmothers had been called either grandmother, grandma, or granny. Whoever heard of calling a grandmother such a strange name?

"I never heard that part of the story, but I do think it's a lovely name. My grandchildren just call me 'Granny,' and I don't feel like I'm as blessed as that sweet woman."

"Sweet? So you met her?" Julia was fascinated by the story of the how the town got its name. She wanted to know everything she could about her new home. Hopefully the older woman would provide her with more information.

"Well, no, but anyone who has a name like 'Wiggie' must be very sweet." Mrs. Davis leaned back in her seat and rested her head against the back. "I've been living in Fort Worth for years, and I have to say, it's a great deal more civilized than Mineral Wells. I hate having to go so far to see my grandchildren, but they just don't come to see me as often as I'd like. These old bones aren't meant for traveling."

Julia smiled. "I'm glad you get to go see them, though." She wished she'd had more time to spend with her own grandmother before her death. She'd died when Julia was just six, though, so she had very few memories of her. Her other grandmother had died long before she was born, so she felt as if she'd missed out on an important part of her childhood.

Mrs. Davis nodded happily. "So am I. I just wish I could see them in Fort Worth instead of Mineral Wells."

"Is Mineral Wells a bad place?" Julia asked. She'd never heard of the place, so she had no idea of anything about it.

"Oh, of course not. It's a perfectly lovely place. The waters there even have healing properties for those who drink them. Many people travel there just to partake of the waters. It's just...not home." Mrs. Davis shrugged one delicate shoulder. "I like to bake for my grandchildren and spoil them rotten. It's not an easy thing to do in another woman's kitchen."

"Are they your son's children or your daughter's children?"

"It would be so much easier if they were my daughter's children, but no, they're my son's."

Julia smiled. She understood the problem with mother-in-law and daughter-in-law, because she'd seen the animosity between her friend and mother-in-law. "I understand. I hope you have a lovely visit." It was obviously important to the older woman to have a good time with her grandchildren, so she wanted everything to work out well for her.

"Oh, I shall. My grandchildren and my son are lovely people. I can't help but have a nice time there."

Julia cover her mouth with her gloved hand to hide her giggle. She couldn't help but notice that the woman didn't include her daughter-in-law with the 'lovely people.' "This is my first teaching assignment, and I'm very excited to get started." She hoped the other woman wouldn't notice her abrupt subject change.

Mrs. Davis smiled. "I taught for a few years when I was younger. *Much* younger."

"You did? Do you have any tips for me?" Julia was always eager to learn from experienced teachers. She had gained a great deal of insight by asking just that question to every teacher she'd ever met.

"Start out strict. You can always be less strict if the children are already well-behaved, but it never works to get stricter with them," Mrs. Davis offered. She continued to give sage advice about teaching until they pulled into Wiggieville. "You're going to do very well, I think."

Julia smiled. "I certainly hope so. I'm very nervous." She really couldn't decide if she was more excited or nervous. Both seemed to be taking up equal parts of her emotions.

"Don't let the children see that or it will be over before it has even begun."

"Thank you for your advice. I will take it all to heart. I so appreciate you talking to me during the drive here." Julia stepped down onto the ground and raised a hand in a wave to the older woman as the stage moved away. She looked around her, trying to find Mr. Hanson, the school board member who had promised to be waiting for her.

THOMAS WAITED ANXIOUSLY in the mercantile for the stage to arrive. His bride, his Anna Simmons, would be on it, and he'd take her right to the pastor's house and marry her. He'd been waiting for a long time to be in a position to be able to marry, and now that he was there, it felt like the wait for her to actually arrive was interminable.

He was a rancher outside of the tiny Texas town of Wiggieville, which was right between Weatherford and Mineral Wells. He'd sent off for a mail order bride, knowing there were just not enough women in Texas. When he'd received Anna's first letter just six weeks before, he'd known immediately she was the wife for him. She seemed very intelligent, and had professed to be a wonderful cook.

When the stage pulled up, he knew immediately the woman coming down was his own sweet Anna. She'd warned him that she was incredibly shy, and she wasn't certain, once she arrived, if she'd be able to go through with it. He'd decided his plan of action, and every time she seemed to be trying to talk him out of marrying her, he'd just kiss her. It would work beautifully.

He caught her eye and walked across the street toward her, so happy to see her in Wiggieville at last. She was a true beauty with her red hair swept atop her head, with a few tendrils falling down out of the knot she had them arranged in. He couldn't see her eye color from the distance he was at, but he didn't think he needed to. He knew he'd never seen a woman who was more attractive to him than the one standing beside the stage.

A tall, handsome man stepped walked across the street toward her, his eyes filled with excitement. He was dark with hair that was almost black and the brownest eyes she'd ever seen. When he reached her, he gave her a very familiar look that startled her. "Are you Miss Simmons?" he asked.

She nodded, holding her hand out to shake his. When he took her hand, he gently pulled her toward him, leaning down to press his lips against hers. She was startled and put her hand to her lips as soon as he pulled back. She knew Texas wasn't as formal as New York, but she'd never expected to be greeted with a kiss, especially not in the middle of the street. What if one of her pupils saw her?

She stepped back, out of his reach, and smiled nervously. "Will you take me to where I'll be staying please?" She decided not to mention the kiss and give him the dressing down he deserved. He was a school board member after all, and as such he needed to be treated with respect, whether he deserved it or not.

He shrugged. "I'd be happy to. We just need to make one stop first, and then we'll be able to head out to the ranch." That stop would, of course, be to the local pastor's house. He just wasn't about to admit it and make her more skittish than she already seemed to be.

Julia frowned. The way she'd understood it, she'd be staying close to the schoolhouse, which would be much better for her, but she could walk if she needed to. "All right." She had no idea what kind of errand he was going to have to run, but she was happy to tag along as long as it didn't take too long. She was excited to go see the schoolhouse and make sure everything was in order. Teaching had been a lifelong dream, and she was finally almost there.

He took her bags from her and held them in one hand, his hand taking hers and pulling her down the street with the other. He seemed to be a man of few words, but that was all right with Julia. She wasn't here to become friendly with the man, just to stay with his family during her year of teaching at the local school. If she liked it, maybe she would even sign another contract and come back the following year.

He stopped to put her belongings into an old farm wagon before pulling her along to a house that was just down the street. He went to the door and knocked loudly, smiling down at her, his grin very impish.

"Where exactly are we?" she asked softly. She didn't want to argue with the man, but something felt wrong about the whole situation. Why was he taking her to someone's house?

Thomas chuckled and leaned down and kissed her again, without answering her. He couldn't believe his sweet bride kept asking him where they were. Had she forgotten she'd traveled all the way from Beckham, Massachusetts to marry him?

Julia felt a tingle run down her spine, wondering what this man was about. She'd been taught to slap any man who just kissed her, but *his* kisses? All she could think about was kissing him back. Her mother would be appalled. What was wrong with her? She'd been raised with better morals than this!

The door opened and a short middle-aged man with silver streaking his brown hair and dancing blue eyes opened the door. "Am I interrupting?" he asked, his eyes twinkling.

Thomas lifted his head, feeling slightly embarrassed at being caught kissing his bride by the reverend. "Reverend this is my bride. Anna Simmons." He grinned down at her as if she were some sort of treasure he'd found.

She looked at Thomas, shaking her head. Anna Simmons? His bride? She tried to pull her hand from his. "No, I'm Julia Simmons." Why was he planning to marry a woman he'd obviously never met? What was wrong with him?

Thomas frowned. Had he gotten her first name wrong? How had he done that? "I'm sorry. Julia Simmons." He'd check the letters once they got home. He was sure she'd said Anna. Maybe she was called by her middle name.

"But, I can't marry you." She couldn't marry a man she'd met only a few minutes before! His kisses turned her brain to mush, but that wasn't enough reason to marry him. And why did he keep kissing her anyway?

Thomas looked at the reverend. "Give me just a minute with my bride, Reverend. We'll just come in when we're ready." He reached out and closed the door, turning back to Julia. "I know you must be nervous, sweetheart." He did the only thing he could think to do to calm her nerves, pulling her to him and kissing her passionately. It was no hardship for him. He could have kept kissing her all day. He could have done a lot more if they weren't in such a public place, and the pastor wasn't waiting for them on the other side of the door.

Julia clung to his shoulders. She didn't know why this man kept kissing her, but she loved his kisses too much to worry about why. Never had a man kissed her as he did, and she enjoyed every second of it. She didn't know why he thought he was supposed to marry her, and he seemed to kiss her every time she tried to talk to him, but she had to make one last effort. "I'm not here to..." She was cut off again by another kiss. He made her feel so many things she'd never felt before that she didn't know what to say.

She stared at him in a daze as he lifted his head.

"Are you ready, sweetheart?" Thomas kept his voice soft, knowing that his new bride was skittish. Once they'd tied the knot, though, everything would be better. She was more beautiful than he'd dreamed she would be, and he couldn't believe his luck finding such a pretty young woman to be his bride. She was everything he'd hoped for and so much more.

She nodded, unsure of anything any longer. She followed him into the house and stood before the reverend with him, repeating her vows as she was told. "You may now kiss the bride." Julia's eyes widened as she heard the words. Had she really just married a stranger? She hadn't even caught his name during the ceremony. What on earth had she done?

Chapter 2

THE REVEREND SHOOK the man's hand. "Congratulations, Tom. I think she's going to make you very happy."

Julia stood looking between the two men trying to figure out what had just happened. Obviously, she'd married Tom, but why? Her brain was more than a little muddled from 'Tom's' kisses. Well, at least she knew her husband's first name now?

Tom took her hand and led her to the wagon, helping her up. "There, that wasn't so bad, now was it?" he asked. He was thrilled to have gotten the ceremony over with.

She looked at him for a moment. "I'm not who you think I am." The words were soft, but she had to say them. He didn't seem to listen to anything she said to him, so she wasn't certain why she was even trying again, but she had to make him understand.

He sighed, releasing the brake on the wagon and starting the horses. "Why are you not who I think you are? You aren't my bride?" Was she going to try and run off for an annulment now that they'd married? Couldn't she just do what she'd promised to do without making things difficult? He took a deep breath, remembering what she'd said about her overwhelming shyness. He had to make concessions for that.

She shook her head. "I've been on trains for ten days. I came here from New York to be the new school teacher." There, she'd finally gotten the words out.

"No, you came here from Beckham, Massachusetts to be my bride. You wrote me a letter." He couldn't believe she was still arguing with him. She didn't seem as shy as he'd expected, but she seemed plenty obstinate.

"I've been writing letters to the head of the school board here, but never to you. I'm Julia Simmons from New York City. I've lived there my entire life, and I've never even heard of Beckham, Massachusetts." Why wouldn't he listen to her? Was he muddled in the head even before their kisses?

He patted her thigh. "You warned me in your letters that you'd be nervous and probably try to get out of marrying me, because you're so shy. It's fine, sweetheart. The wedding is over."

He wasn't going to believe anything she said, and as they drove, she got more and more panicky. "I need to teach at the school in Wiggieville on Monday morning." Surely he would take her back to town now that she'd said that. She could get an annulment and everything would be good.

He sighed. "You'll meet the school board members at church on Sunday. It'll all be just fine." He'd humor her if it would make her be less worried. He'd thought he was past her apprehensions when she said "I do," but they seemed to just go on and on.

She watched the scenery as they drove, but said little else. He obviously wasn't going to listen to her, so she wasn't going to waste her breath arguing with him.

When they pulled into a yard in front of a large wooden house, he jumped down and walked around to help her down. Once she was on the ground, he leaned down and kissed her again, and even though he was making her crazy by not listening to her, she responded immediately to his kiss. Her heart beat faster, and her knees felt weak. He had a power over her that she couldn't deny.

He wrapped her in his arms, knowing it was the key to settling her down, and pulled her against him, kissing her passionately. He slowly traced her lips with his tongue, and when she parted her lips in response, he took advantage by moving his tongue in to mate with hers.

She felt a jolt of energy run through her body and grabbed his shoulders, clinging to him. Suddenly she wasn't certain if her legs could support her, as she stood beside the wagon, pressing her body to his.

Whatever drove her crazy about this man, when he kissed her, her insides turned to mush.

Tom cupped her backside in his hands pulling her against him. He knew she would probably want to wait until bedtime to consummate the marriage, but with her obvious flightiness, he didn't think that was a good idea. "Let me put the horses in their stalls, and I'll show you around." *Show you my bedroom.*

He worked quickly, getting the horses unhitched from the wagon and rubbing them down. Keeping his eyes on her face, every time she looked ready for flight, he'd hurry over and kiss her again until she had that glazed look on her face, and then he'd hurry even faster to get the horses taken care of. It took him twice as long as it should have to unhitch the team because he kissed her so many times.

When he was finished, he walked to her and pulled her into his arms, kissing her again until she couldn't support her weight with her own legs. He scooped her into his arms and carried her toward the house, thinking of nothing but getting her into his bed. He'd known from her letters there would be something special between them, but this level of feeling was beyond anything he'd dreamed of.

She stared up at his face, knowing she needed to try one more time before she just went along with him. "I think there's been a misunderstanding..." she began, and he pressed his lips to hers, standing with her cradled against him, right there on the front porch of his house.

"Don't worry about anything. I'll take care of you," he whispered, opening the door and carrying her inside. He showed her nothing, just carried her straight to the bedroom, laying her on the bed and following her down onto it, propping himself on one elbow beside her. "You're even more beautiful than I imagined you'd be." He traced her cheek with his index finger, still having a hard time believing that this beautiful woman was his wife, and he had every right to kiss her and touch her as much as he wanted.

Julia stared up into his face, surprised that he thought she was beautiful. No one had ever said that about her before. "I'm not beautiful," she protested. He was beautiful though. She'd never seen a more handsome man in her life. He was tall, with dark hair and brown eyes. His eyelashes seemed to go on forever, and his mouth. Her eyes dropped to the mouth that seemed to be kissing her endlessly. It looked hard and chiseled, but she knew better. His lips were soft against hers and oh so loving.

He moved closer to her on the bed, his lips covering hers once more. His kisses made her feel as if her brain could no longer function, and she was happy to give into the bliss of not having to worry about every little thing.

She kissed him back, using her tongue as he'd taught her, wrapping her arms around his hard shoulders. He'd said he was a rancher, so he must work hard every day, making those muscles bulge. She moved her hands around to the front of his shirt, slowly unbuttoning it, because never in her life had she wanted to touch anyone as much as she wanted to touch his bare skin. It was so hot, but she just couldn't make herself care.

Tom was startled to feel her fingers unbuttoning his shirt, but he didn't say a word, because he certainly didn't want her to stop. He moved his hands to the back of her dress and slowly liberated each button from its hole. Once he was finished, his hands roamed over her back, wondering if it would startle her if he pushed her dress off his shoulders. She certainly didn't seem like she was shy.

Part of Julia's mind knew she should protest when he unbuttoned her dress, but she didn't want to. She wanted what he was doing to her more than she'd ever wanted anything, even to teach.

Before she knew what had happened, she was lying beside him totally nude and he was wearing only his pants. He'd even removed his boots during her glaze of passion. Her hands reached out to stroke his bare chest, toying with the light covering of hair and his flat nipples. At his groan, her eyes met his, and she gently rolled the nipples between her fingers, thrilled that he was enjoying what she did to him.

Tom couldn't believe how wild in bed his little wife was turning out to be. She'd claimed to be a schoolteacher, but no teacher he'd ever known would act this way. He cupped her bare breasts in his hands, his thumbs flicking over the nipples, watching her face carefully to see what she enjoyed and what she didn't. As far as he could tell she liked it all.

He lowered his face to her breast, taking her nipple between his lips to suckle it. At her gasp of pleasure, he toyed with the nipple of her other breast, while he flicked his tongue rapidly over the nipple he held in his mouth.

She wove her fingers through his hair, holding his head against her, arching beneath him to get closer. She wanted so much more from this man.

He stroked a path down her stomach and across her hip. His hand moving between her thighs and slowly stroking up the inside to her core. His fingers toyed with her pleasure button for a moment before he plunged one finger into her tight channel. He kissed a path down her stomach, gently biting the skin there.

At her moan of pleasure, he rolled from the bed and stripped out of his pants, quickly pushing them to the floor and rejoining her on the bed, kneeling between her spread thighs. He reached down a hand to guide himself to her opening, his eyes on hers the entire time. He didn't want to hurt her, but he didn't think he could wait another minute. All the kisses they'd shared since they'd met had a huge effect on him.

She was looking into his eyes as he pushed inside her, and she let out a cry of surprise. Yes, it hurt, but only a little. More than anything there was a feeling of fullness, and she liked it. She arched her hips up toward him, hoping to feel the sensation forever.

He slowly drew out of her, watching her face for any sign of panic or pain, but his sweet little innocent bride seemed to want nothing more than to make love with him.

When he pulled from her, Julia tried to follow him up. She wanted all of him to squeeze tightly inside her. She liked it. She needed him. "Don't go!" she whispered.

He slid back into her with ease, grinning down at her lazily as if he had all the time in the world. "I'm not going anywhere, wife."

Afterward, he curled up at her side, cradling her against him. They were both out of breath, but it was done. She couldn't run away and get an annulment now. She was his forever.

She lay with her head on his shoulder, looking at him. "I...I'm not who you think I am. My name is Julia Simmons. I came here to teach school, not to be your wife." She knew that it was too late for either of them to do anything about being married. They would be together forever whether they wanted to be or not, but he still needed to know the truth.

He looked at her for a moment and shook his head. "No, you're my bride." Why was she persisting in telling him she wasn't his?

"I'm not sure how you met your bride that you don't know what she looks like, but I've never heard of Anna Simmons. I was expecting a member of the school board, who said I could live with his family during the school year to meet me at the stage. Instead, you were there not letting me speak. Every time I opened my mouth you kissed me." Her green eyes were wide as they looked into his.

Tom shook his head. It couldn't be true. "So why did you marry me?" That was the only part that made no sense to him. If she hadn't come there to marry him, why had she said her vows?

"Every time I tried to protest you started kissing me, and...well your kisses turned my brain to mush. I couldn't figure out how to protest." She knew it sounded silly, but it was the only truth she had.

"Well then where's Anna? Was she on the stage with you?" He was confused, but she seemed very sure of herself.

Julia shook her head. "No, she wasn't. It was only me and an elderly woman named Mrs. Davis." She looked at him and frowned. "Do you know I don't even know your last name? Or mine, I guess..." How could she not know her own last name? What was wrong with her?

"Harding. Thomas Harding." He felt like he should shake her hand, but he'd just shaken the bed with her, so that wouldn't work. "I...uh...I'm not sure what I should say. I'm sorry I didn't let you explain." He hoped she didn't have a beau waiting on her to come home after her time teaching in Wiggieville, but he was too afraid of her answer to even ask her that.

She shook her head. "I should have tried harder, but...every time you kissed me, I lost my ability to speak." She blushed as she said the words, truly surprised that she could still be embarrassed around him after what they'd just done together.

"You...I mean Anna, wrote to me that she was really shy and would probably lose her nerve when she got here. She was afraid she'd try to talk me out of it or run off. I thought you were just being shy and doing what she'd said you'd do, or she'd do, I guess, so I...well...I kept kissing you to give you courage and pushed you along, thinking that's what I was supposed to do." He shook his head, angry with himself that he'd messed things up so badly.

Julia let out a short bark of laughter. "Well, it worked! I don't think there's anything we can do about it now, either. I mean, if you'd let me explain before, we could have gotten an annulment." They couldn't get one now, though, and she found she wasn't terribly upset about it. He seemed like a good man, and she did enjoy his touch.

"I was so worried about it that I rushed things." He eyed her. "How are you going to teach, clean, *and* cook?" He had no idea how she would be able to get everything done, but he needed her to be the wife he'd expected. They were married now, and he couldn't just marry someone else to do the housework.

She sighed. "I have no idea. This was my first teaching assignment and I was so excited about it." She didn't know what would happen now. She knew many places didn't allow their teachers to be married.

"You were my first wife, and I was just as excited." He grinned ruefully. "I hope you're my only wife."

She sighed, moving closer to him. "I hope so too." She refused to worry about anything else. "You said I'd meet the school board on Sunday, and I will. Until then, I'll concentrate on settling in and being a good wife I guess." She pressed a kiss to his chin.

Tom smiled, stroking her cheek. "How would you feel about resigning your post and just being my wife?" He knew her answer before he even asked, because she was obviously very excited about being a teacher, but he had to at least try.

Julia sat up in the bed, oblivious to the fact that she was totally naked and had dropped the sheet to her waist. "I can't do that! I'm a teacher. I've taken so many tests, and I've studied so hard for this privilege. I need to at least teach my first year." She couldn't let her parents down that way.

Tom frowned. This certainly wasn't working out as he'd planned. "All right. You can work at least this year." He sat up, swinging his legs over the side of the bed and gathering his clothes to put them on. He wasn't sure why he felt betrayed when she wanted to keep teaching but he did. "We'll figure it all out. Let me show you around the house."

As soon as she realized he was dressing with his back to her, Julia flew out of the bed and pulled her clothes on as quickly as she could. The house was big, much bigger than the tenement she'd lived in growing up.

Both of her parents had worked in factories but had felt that she needed to go to school. Most of the children she knew were already working in the factories by the time they were fourteen, but her parents had insisted she complete her education so she could be a teacher. They'd made a great deal of sacrifices for her, and what had she done? She'd ruined them all by marrying a man who she'd never met as soon as she stepped off the stage.

Once she was dressed, she turned around to see him watching her. He walked to her and kissed her softly. "I know this wasn't how you'd planned to spend the day, so I'm sorry this happened. I'm thrilled to have you for my wife, though. You're exactly what I'd dreamed Anna would be like and so much more." More was definitely the truth. He didn't know how he would have done with such a shy woman, but he hadn't been about to turn down the opportunity to marry. He needed to marry. It was time.

Julia blushed. She honestly wasn't sorry she'd married him either. He was a nice-looking man who had a great personality. How could she possibly complain about that?

Chapter 3

JULIA STOOD IN THE large kitchen looking around her. His parents had lived in the house with him and had recently moved back East. It was their departure that had made him decide he needed a wife, he'd told her.

She searched through the small pantry for something to make for supper. She found some salt pork and potatoes and carrots. They could easily be used to make a tasty stew. They would need to shop for provisions within a day or two, because she wouldn't be able to cook all day every day, but she was determined to make it work. She'd made her bed and she'd lain in it as well. It was time to fulfill her obligations.

She started the stew and looked around the room, noticing the dust everywhere. She had a big job ahead of her when it came to cooking and cleaning, and she would do her very best to get it in shape before school started, because after, she would have a great deal to do, being gone all day five days per week, and having to catch up on the cleaning on Saturdays. She was tired just thinking about it.

When Tom came back in from the range, he took a deep sniff of the aromas coming from the pot on top of the stove and glanced around him. She'd only had two hours alone in the house, and it was already cleaner than it had been in a year. She'd scrubbed the floors and every surface. Even the windows were shining.

He searched until he found her in his bedroom, the only bedroom on the first floor of the house, and she was there, making the bed with the spare set of sheets. How nice. He couldn't remember the last time he'd thought to change the sheets.

She turned and gave him a wary glance, biting her lip as she looked at him. He walked to her and pulled her into his arms, kissing her softly. "I know you weren't planning to be a wife, so I thank you for the hard work you put in here today." She was obviously working hard to do what she thought was right.

Julia nodded at him, smiling tentatively. "This is...awkward." It felt strange to be around a man she'd been so...uninhibited with.

He laughed, pulling her into his arms and kissing her. "It's only awkward when we're not kissing. What do you think about spending all of our time kissing and lounging in bed?" He certainly liked the idea, but there was a good chance they'd go broke and starve to death. He wasn't certain he cared at that moment, though.

She laughed softly. "I'm not certain that's a good idea. Someone needs to make a living." She pressed a kiss to his cheek, though, amazed at just how tall he was. She'd always been tall, and to have a man a good five inches taller than she was as a husband was truly a dream come true.

"My idea is fun, though." He nipped at her neck, not really trying to convince her, but enjoying her struggles. "Probably not practical." He pulled away. "I do appreciate how hard you've worked today."

She smiled and nodded. "I made a stew for supper. I hope you like stew." She could see that she'd be making a lot of soups and stews, because they would be easier after working all day.

He shrugged. "As long as someone is cooking for me, I'm happy. I only knew how to make a few meals."

She led him into the kitchen, and the big table with six chairs sitting around it. "Were you an only child?" She'd always wished for brothers and sisters, but it just hadn't happened for her.

He shook his head. "I have three sisters. They're all married now. One moved to Fort Worth, one lives in Mineral Wells, and the other is in Weatherford."

"And none of them came to the wedding?"

"I didn't tell them I was getting married. I'll introduce you at Christmas when we'll all get together. Ma and Pa said they'd be here for Christmas as well." He looked forward to introducing her to his family. He couldn't believe the overwhelming sense of pride he had for her.

She wondered where his parents would stay. She knew there were four bedrooms upstairs, but she had yet to see them. She had decided that taking care of the rooms they would use the most needed to be her first order of business. Besides, it was much hotter upstairs than down. She really didn't want to have to climb up there in the heat. The Texas summer was more than hot enough for her when she was downstairs.

"They'll probably stay with my oldest sister, Sarah. She has four children for them to dote on." He watched her as she served them each a bowl of the stew.

"How did you know I was wondering that?" She didn't like to think that her thoughts were so transparent to him.

He shrugged. "I just did. I know most women don't have good relationships with their mother-in-laws." She put his stew on the table in front of him and poured the water from the pitcher he had sitting on the counter. "That water is mineral water, from Mineral Wells. It's supposed to have good health effects. My sister sent some home with me the last time I visited." He didn't know that he agreed with the health benefits, but he was happy to drink it just in case.

Julia looked at him with surprise. "Really? How nice." She thought it was nice that his sister thought of him that way.

She brought them each a glass of water before sitting across from him. He bowed his head for the prayer and she followed suit. Her family hadn't been very religious, often times skipping church altogether, but she certainly knew how to pray, and if it made him happy, she would do it.

"Do you have any brothers and sisters?" he asked, realizing he knew absolutely nothing about her.

She shook her head. "No, it was just me. My parents worked in textile factories in the city." She knew a lot of people looked down on factory workers, but she was proud that her parents had worked so hard to give her a good life. How could she ever look down on them?

"And you went to school there?" He'd never lived in a big city, but he knew without a doubt that she would have a lot of adjusting to do to get used to a small town like Wiggieville.

She nodded. "I loved school. I always have. It was my parents' dream for me to never step foot in a factory, and instead, to go out West and teach. So I did this to make them happy." She didn't add that somewhere along the way it had become her dream as well, because she knew that much was already clear to him. She didn't want him to feel any worse than he already did about pushing so hard to get her to marry him.

"And I messed it up for you."

She shook her head. "I wouldn't say that. They wanted me to marry and have children. They just wanted me to teach for a while first." She didn't add that a while was a minimum of five years in her parents' eyes. She was not looking forward to their reaction when she wrote to them to explain what had happened.

He sighed. "I really am sorry I didn't let you explain." He felt like a heel, coming on so strong and not letting her get in a word.

She laughed. "Maybe it was meant to be? How many Miss Simmons were supposed to get off that stage today? It's very odd." Her name was common, but it wasn't so common that she was constantly running into other people with her name. She believed very much in fate, though, and if it was her fate to be a bride instead of a teacher, then she would do what she needed to do.

"It is." He fought to find the right words to say what he wanted to say. "I'm glad you're the Miss Simmons who got off the train today and not Anna. I don't think there could be a woman who would suit me better." His eyes bored into hers as he spoke, and he hoped they conveyed even a fraction of his feelings.

She blushed. "Even though I'm going to be working five days a week?" She knew that he didn't want her working, but she also knew that she would fulfill her obligations, both to her parents and to the town.

He frowned. "I'm honestly not very happy about that, but we'll make it work. I have an old buggy in the barn that was driven by my mother and sisters when they needed to go to town. Pa didn't like them taking the wagon. I'll hitch it up for you five mornings a week, and you can drive it to school and back home." He didn't like the idea of her being gone so much, but it was what she'd agreed to do, so he understood.

She smiled nodding. "I can do that." She was thankful he was looking for solutions to make teaching possible for her instead of trying to keep her from being able to do it. Most men wouldn't want their wives to work and would actively try to prevent it from happening.

After supper she did the dishes in silence, not knowing what to say to this stranger she suddenly found herself married to. He made her crazy at times, not listening to her and pushing her to do things she didn't want to do, but in bed? He made her body sing. She'd never experienced anything like what she felt when he took her into his arms. What was it about him? Other boys had tried to steal kisses from her, but she'd firmly stomped on their feet or slapped their faces. With him? She melted. Her brain turned to mush and her legs stopped working. She was suddenly unable to think on her own. She became his as soon as he touched his lips to hers.

"Do you want to get a bath before bed tonight?" he asked, thinking she must feel dirty after so many days on a train.

She nodded. "That would be fabulous. Where's the tub?" she asked. She would start heating water as soon as she'd finished the dishes.

He looked at her for a moment. "You really didn't explore the house much, did you?"

"I didn't think I should take the time. I started supper, and did some cleaning. I only worked in here and in the bedroom. I never even made it into the parlor to clean in there." She gave him a questioning glance.

He smiled and led her through the house, up the stairs, to a closed door. Opening it for her, he let her precede him inside the tiny room. It only held three things. A commode, a wash basin, and a bathtub. A porcelain bathtub, that had running water. She squealed and started the tap. "I've never even seen one of these!" She'd heard of them, though, and had desperately wanted to try one out.

"My mother insisted, so my father put one in. It's the only real luxury I have to offer, but I think it's a good one." He was pleased by the excitement on her face for his surprise.

"Oh my, yes. It's a very good one!" She stood on tiptoes and kissed him quickly. "I'm so excited!" She couldn't wait to take a bath where no one had had to carry water. It was a wonderful surprise indeed.

He laughed, turning her around so he could unbutton her dress. "You enjoy your bath. There are towels in that cabinet. If you need me, all you have to do is call."

She made a face as he left, closing the door behind him. Quickly she shucked off her clothes and climbed into the bathtub, leaning back against it and sighing. A real bathtub with running water. It was a luxury she certainly hadn't been expecting to find in Texas of all places.

As she soaked, she thought about the strange turn her day had taken. How could she have messed up her first teaching assignment so badly? Marrying a random stranger as soon as you get off the stage was not something a good school teacher did. She hoped they wouldn't try to keep her from teaching.

Chapter 4

SUNDAY MORNING AT CHURCH, Tom introduced Julia to the head of the school board, Timothy Hanson. When he saw her, he was confused. "But you sent a telegram saying you'd be two weeks late."

Julia shook her head. "No, I didn't. When did I send that?" He thought he'd received a telegram from her? No wonder Tom had been the only one waiting for her.

He dug into his pocket. "See? Right here." He handed her the telegram. "TH I will be arriving two weeks later than scheduled stop I hope you will forgive me for making everyone wait stop Miss Simmons stop"

Julia almost laughed before handing the telegram to Tom. "She'll be here in two weeks apparently." She hoped that Tom would still want to remain married to her after Anna arrived.

Tom read it and shook his head. "This is ridiculous. If I'd actually gotten this telegram, I wouldn't have pushed you into marrying me." He couldn't believe that the telegram had been misplaced that way.

Mr. Hanson looked between the two of them. "So you married Thomas instead of waiting for me?" His face was incredulous.

Julia blushed, shaking her head. "Honestly, it was all very confusing. You see Tom sent for a mail order bride, and she was supposed to arrive on the same stage as me. Her name was Anna Simmons. I'm Julia Simmons, and when Tom saw me, he asked if I was Miss Simmons, so he assumed I was here to marry him when I said 'yes.' He was the only person waiting for me, so I thought he was from the school board." She knew that didn't make much sense, but she wasn't going to explain that Tom's kisses made her lose her senses. That would make her look like someone she didn't want to be.

Mr. Hanson frowned. "I'm still not sure how that would have led to a marriage, but I can see that it did. You'll have to resign, of course."

Julia shook her head. "But why? I can be a wife and a teacher at the same time." She hoped he would listen to reason. She'd worked too hard to become a teacher to have her plans thwarted now.

"It just isn't done. I suppose I can let you stay on until a new teacher is found, and it will be nice not having to postpone the start of school like we thought, but really, we couldn't let you teach the whole year. We'll find someone to take your place." Mr. Hanson turned and walked away, and Julia knew better than to argue. There had been a definite air of finality to his words.

She looked at Tom, her eyes sad. "I guess you won't have to put up with a working wife for an entire year after all." She walked over to sit in the pew he'd pointed out as the one he usually sat in and folded her hands in her lap, no longer interested in meeting a lot of new people. She blinked rapidly, doing her best to hold back the tears. What a way to meet new people.

Tom moved beside her and awkwardly patted her hand. "It'll work out. You'll see." He didn't know how it would work out, but he was determined to make it happen.

Several of the children heard she was to be their new teacher and rushed across the room to gawk at her. Only one was bold enough to actually introduce herself, an older girl named Beatrice. "You're the new teacher?" she asked, sitting down beside Julia.

Julia nodded. "I'll be teaching you at least for a short time." She tried to smile, but it felt forced, even to her.

"I love school. My favorite subject is reading, but I like arithmetic and geography almost as much. I just finished reading *Heidi*. Have you read it?"

Julia's eyes lit up. "I borrowed it from my teacher two years ago. It was a wonderful story. What other books have you read?"

Tom grinned, knowing his new wife would be content as she talked to her student for a while. He walked over to Mr. Hanson, talking to him in low tones. "It means a lot to Julia to be able to teach at the school. I don't much want her to do it, but I'd appreciate it if you'd let her at least finish out the year there. Let her work until Christmas and if she's not doing her job well enough, then find someone else then."

Mr. Hanson shook his head. "It clearly states in her contract that she can't be married. We can't have a married schoolteacher. If it were a man maybe, but not a lady. It's just not right."

Tom scratched his head. "I don't see why not. It doesn't make sense to me that you would penalize her for being married. Wouldn't that make her more settled to not be thinking about marrying every eligible man in town?"

"I'm sorry, Tom. We're not going to see eye to eye on this. Finding another teacher will be my first priority." Mr. Hanson turned his back on Tom and strode from the building. He made it clear he wasn't interested in anything else Tom had to say on the matter.

When Tom walked back to the pew he'd shared with Julia, he found her still talking to the girl beside her about books they'd both read. He laughed softly. She would inspire children to read whether she was formally teaching them or not. He'd make sure to tell her that on their way home that afternoon.

As they drove toward the ranch, Tom took her hand in his. "I know you wanted to teach, but I'm not sorry that you're my wife." He looked at her out of the corner of his eye as he watched the road. He didn't want her to regret their marriage.

Julia made a face, but nodded. "I just wish I could be married to you and teach." She knew she didn't regret their marriage either. Every day her feelings for him were a little bit stronger, and she looked forward to the time when she could be a full time wife. She would have preferred that time to only happen during the summers, but she knew that wasn't a possibility any longer. Resting her head on his shoulder, she knew that even though her life was much different than she'd pictured it as she took the train West, she would be happy if she could spend every night in Tom's arms.

Tom was pleased with her answer, but still worried that she wasn't entirely happy. He knew she'd studied hard to get her teacher's certificate, and he hated that he was keeping her from being able to use it. If he'd given her time to explain, maybe he could have courted her and ended up married anyway. He didn't think Anna was ever going to show up, and even if she did, he knew there was no way he could prefer her to his sweet Julia.

JULIA WAS NERVOUS MONDAY morning as she prepared for her first day as a teacher. She had her lunch in a pail, and she had made a large pot of soup, leaving it in the oven to keep it hot while she was at work. Tom could have some for lunch if he wanted, and she would have very little to do to prepare it for their supper once they got home. Not yet knowing how tired she would be after her first day of teaching, she thought that was for the best.

"Would you mind hitching up the buggy for me so I can drive myself to school?" she asked after she'd washed the breakfast dishes. "I don't think I could handle the wagon." He'd offered before, so she was certain he'd just do it when she asked.

Tom looked at her over his coffee cup and finally shook his head. "At least for today, I'm going to drive you into town and pick you up. I don't know what else to do."

She frowned. "I'm sure I could handle the buggy just fine." She didn't want him to think that she needed to be totally dependent on him.

He shrugged. "I'll just feel better if I know you got there safely. It may be crazy, but I'd appreciate it greatly if you'd just let me drive you." He didn't know what he was worried about, except that she would go to school and never come home. He needed to be a part of all of her life, even her teaching.

"That's fine. You can drive me." She didn't want to argue with him about it, but she really would have preferred showing up for her first day on the job alone. Would the children think she was afraid if he drove her?

She picked up her lunch pail and carried it out to the wagon which he had hitched and waiting for her. He helped her up, and she tucked the lap robe around her, not wanting to mess up her skirt. She wanted to look her best for her first day of school with the new children. She'd met several of them at church on Sunday, but she was nervous about the others, of course.

The drive to the schoolhouse took more time than she would like and she found herself pushing her feet against the front of the wagon, as if it would get them there faster. Once she realized what she was doing, she let out a low laugh.

Tom looked at her with surprise. "What's so funny?" She'd seemed nervous until she'd laughed, so he had no idea what was going on in her mind.

Julia grinned and nodded at her feet. "I'm so excited about my first day teaching that I'm actually pushing my feet against the front of the wagon like it will get us there faster."

He laughed softly, his arm going around her shoulders. "I'm glad you are happy to be going. I know it took them a while to find you to teach. You may be able to teach here for a few months before they can replace you." As much as he wanted her home full time, he wanted her to be happy, and her feelings were more important to him than his own.

Julia smiled, resting her head against his shoulder, before realizing she could muss up her hair. She sat up straight, and felt the sides to make sure none of her hair had fallen from her bun. "I would really like that. I know you want a full time wife, though."

He shrugged. "It was my mistake that led you to change your life for me. I know that you'd like to teach for as long as you can. I won't begrudge you the time with the children."

She looked at him and smiled. He was truly a good man, and she couldn't be unhappy that she was fortunate enough to have married him. "I appreciate you saying that. It makes me feel so much better about it."

"I don't want you to be unhappy because you don't get to do what you dreamed of doing. I hope you enjoy teaching as much as you think you will."

"Thank you. I hope so, too." She held her books and lunch pail in her lap as he pulled up in front of the school. She waited until he walked around to her side of the wagon and helped her down. They'd arrived a good half hour before school was to start, and she was thankful for that.

He went into the schoolhouse with her, planning to chase away any critters that had taken up residence there over the summer. When he saw how clean it was, he was surprised. "Someone came and cleaned up for you, I see."

She nodded, walking to the teacher's desk and running her hand across it. She walked to the windows and opened them all one by one. They would need the breeze if the children were going to try to pay attention at all. September in Texas was a lot hotter than September in New York. She sat down at her desk and looked in the drawers. Someone had slipped pencils and paper into the drawers, and she was very thankful. She had everything she needed to start her day.

"Do you need me to do anything for you before I leave?" he asked. He didn't want to leave her in town, but he knew this was where she needed to be.

She shook her head. "I'll be fine. I guess I'll see you at four."

"I'll be here." He walked to the door and turned back to look at her sitting at the teacher's desk with a huge smile lighting up her face, and he felt more than a little guilty. She was where she wanted to be. He wished he hadn't messed up her plans so badly.

Julia looked at the small clock on her desk and realized it hadn't been wound. She carefully set the time and wound the clock, setting it to the time on the watch pinned to her breast. She noted that she only had five minutes before it would be time to call the children in. There was a small bell on her desk that she would use to let the children know it was time for classes to start. Her palms were sweaty as she thought of the day ahead. She would have to mainly learn about her students the first day, and she was looking forward to it, but nervous at the same time. They would start the in-depth learning the following day.

She went to the door and rang the bell, noting that the schoolyard was sparse. There were small boys and girls of all ages. As Beatrice walked past her toward her desk, Julia stopped her. "Where are the bigger boys?" she asked.

"Oh, they'll be coming later in the year. They need to help with round up and getting the crops in. Most of them are only here from mid-October through March." Beatrice hurried to her desk and took her seat, sitting with a girl around her age whom Julia hadn't met yet.

Julia walked to her desk and picked up a notebook, turning it to the first page. "I need to get everyone's names and ages please. If you know where you are in your readers, please let me know. I'll walk around the room and talk to each of you individually. You may whisper quietly while I do this. If anyone gets out of hand, I will take away the privilege of whispering." She wanted to be nice but firm with the children, letting them know they wouldn't get away with a lot of shenanigans in her classroom.

She walked around the room and took the names of all the students. There were only fourteen of them, but there was room for six more. "How many older boys are part of your class?" she asked.

Ann Hayes, one of the girls in the back row, raised her hand. "There are just four."

"Do they do any studies when they're not in school?" Julia asked. She hated that the older boys were in school for such a short period every year, but she knew it was the way things were done in most places.

Ann shook her head. "No, ma'am. Most boys around here will be farmers or ranchers anyway. There's no reason for them to go to school when they can learn their trades at home." Ann was a tall thin girl with blond hair and blue eyes. She was about fifteen and wore her hair in a bun atop her head.

Julia nodded, not wanting to argue with the common thoughts about educating boys. She knew she wouldn't win anyway. "I see you're already sitting divided into classes. I'll write the assignments on the board for you to study for everyone but the first reader group, and I'll work with them at my desk. Everyone else, please work quietly." She found she was much less nervous than she expected to be now that the time was at hand for her to actually teach. The students sat before her with their hands folded, and they began work immediately. Someone had trained them very well to pay attention and do what they were told during class.

The day progressed very well for Julia. The children were well-behaved, and the day moved quickly. At lunch time, several of the older girls asked if they may stay inside so they could work on the knitting and crocheting they'd brought with them. Julia granted them permission and watched them as she ate her lunch, wishing she was allowed to sit with them. She was only eighteen, and at least two of her students were within a year or two of her age. She couldn't become too friendly with them, though, because she couldn't risk forming a close friendship with a student and losing her authority.

At the end of the day, as she watched her students leave, Julia felt slightly let down. She'd loved the work, but she had hoped she would change the world of at least one of her students. She knew that this group had been trained well by former teachers and none of them really needed their world changed.

She dismissed the students at four and quickly swept the classroom, making certain everything was clean and ready for the next day. She had just finished up and was closing the windows when she spotted Tom driving up. She took her bonnet from the hook behind her desk and carefully tied it under her chin. It wouldn't be good for her to seem unkempt around town while she was the schoolteacher.

Chapter 5

"HOW'S THE TEACHER TODAY?" Tom asked after helping her into the wagon. As much as he hated that she was away all day, he was proud of her for what she did.

She sighed. "It was a good day. I'm exhausted, but I think everything went well. All the students were very well behaved."

"You sound like that's a bad thing." He looked at her questioningly as he sat down and took the reins. "Did something bad happen?"

Julia shook her head. "Nothing bad happened at all." She knew her voice sounded disappointed, but she wasn't sure how to stop it from sounding that way.

"And that makes you sad?"

"I was hoping that my first day would be going into class and finding out that all of my students desperately needed me to change their lives. I wanted one of them to have trouble learning or have trouble at home where they needed me. Instead, I have a classroom full of well-behaved students who are right where they should be educationally. The only real problem is that the older boys aren't there, but that's nothing unusual. It wasn't like that in my school, but it's normal in rural areas from what I understand."

He laughed softly. "You realize you're upset because there were no problems, right?"

She shrugged. "I wanted to change the world with my teaching, or if not the entire world at least one child's world."

He squeezed her hand. "I'm sorry it wasn't what you expected it to be."

"It's all right. I won't be doing it for very long anyway. At least I was able to do some teaching." She hated to admit that she was disappointed in her day, but she really was. She didn't know why she wanted to have troubled students, but that's what she'd always imagined she'd be facing. Now she would just have to get used to the fact that she wouldn't have her well-behaved students for long.

WHEN JULIA LEFT THE school on the Friday of her second week as a teacher, she drove the buggy past the stagecoach. As the stage pulled away, there was a young woman standing looking around bewilderedly, obviously searching for something. She could see the other woman had tears in her eyes so she pulled over and asked, "Are you here to meet someone?"

The girl nodded. "I'm here to meet my fiancé, Tom Harding. He was supposed to be waiting for me."

Julia felt her heart fall into her stomach. She knew there was only one thing she could do, so she did it immediately. "Come with me. We'll talk." She waited as the other woman threw her bags into the back of the buggy, and grabbing a handhold, climbed up to join her. "My name is Julia."

"I'm Anna Simmons." Her voice was soft, and she looked so sweet sitting there beside her, making Julia wish that Tom could have had her for his wife. He deserved someone soft spoken and sweet, unlike her.

"I was Julia Simmons until two weeks ago. I'm going to tell you a funny story." At Anna's nod, Julia told the story of her arriving and Tom confirming she was 'Miss Simmons.' She told her how she kept trying to protest, but how Tom had just kissed her every time. "And that's how I ended up married to your fiancé."

Anna made a face. "I can certainly understand how that could have happened. I told him I was certain that once I arrived, I would just try to run back home, so he must have just kept kissing you to keep you from running away." She shrugged. "I'm not upset, because he was a stranger to me, but I don't know what I'm supposed to do now."

Julia smiled at the other woman. "Well, I think there's only one answer. You go home with me." They had a spare room she could put her in, and Anna could decide what to do from there. They could use her first month's wages to send her back to Massachusetts if they needed to.

"So what's Tom like?" Anna asked, her face devoid of expression.

Julia grinned. "He's a wonderful husband to me. I honestly couldn't ask for a better man. I'm still teaching until another teacher can be found, and he's been very supportive of me throughout it all." She didn't add that she was certain she would lose him to Anna. She didn't want anyone to know how insecure he was, but if he could fall in love with her as soon as he saw her just thinking she was Anna, how would he feel when he saw the real woman?

"Will he mind that you're bringing me home with you?" Anna looked nervous at the idea.

Julia shook her head. "No, of course not. He'll understand that he's the one who stranded you by marrying me, so it's our responsibility to help you. We have a spare room that you can use until you decide what you want to do." It would be strange having the other woman living in their house, even for a short period, but she didn't feel like she could do anything else.

Anna bit her lip. "I guess I really have nowhere to go, do I?"

"We would buy you a ticket back home if you need us to, or there are plenty of unmarried men around. You could stay with us until you found one you were interested in marrying. Or you don't happen to be a certified teacher do you?" She knew it was a long shot, but it would be great if they could just switch roles. She'd married Anna's fiancé, so maybe Anna could teach in her place.

Anna looked at her in surprise. "I was a teacher before I left home. Why? Does this town need a teacher now?"

Julia looked at Anna with surprise. Hadn't she listened to anything she'd said? "They don't allow married women to teach here, so I'm just working until they find someone to replace me. If you wanted to teach, you would have a place to stay, because there was a family in town who had agreed to let me board there." She looked at the other woman questioningly, hoping that she was willing to take her place.

Anna nodded, obviously thinking about it. "Could you introduce me to the school board at church on Sunday? If you don't mind that is."

"Oh, I don't mind at all. Mr. Hanson will be pleased to have someone interested in the post, because he's very eager to get rid of me." Julia shrugged. "He really has a problem with a married woman teaching, but I'm not certain why. I've never really understood why a married woman can't be as good of a teacher as an unmarried woman. I'd think a married woman would be more focused on the students and not thinking nearly as much about who she's going to marry."

"I'm not certain I understand the reasoning either, but I do know it's a rule in most places." Anna looked out the window. "How far is it to the ranch?"

"We're almost there. Tom doesn't know you're coming, so be prepared for him to be surprised. He never got your telegram, you know. It went to Mr. Hanson, because you just used initials, and Tom and Mr. Hanson have the same initials." She grinned as she mentioned the mix up. She knew she shouldn't find it amusing, but if it hadn't happened, she never would have married Tom.

"I guess I did everything wrong, didn't I? If I'd gotten on that train the day I was supposed to instead of being too afraid to leave town, none of this ever would have happened."

"Oh, is that why you were late?" Julia parked in front of the ranch house, and carefully stepped down. She picked up her books and lunch pail to carry inside. "If you want to leave your bags, Tom will happily take them in for you when he unhitches the horse." She patted the horse's neck as she walked toward the house.

Julia hurried inside and immediately went to the kitchen. She hadn't yet started supper, and now she had three mouths to feed instead of two. When she turned, she saw that Anna had donned her apron and had set her bags on the floor beside the table. Julia smiled. "You don't have to help with supper. Your room is at the top of the stairs. Go ahead and get comfortable." She didn't want their guest to have to help cook.

"Oh, I love to cook," Anna protested. "What are you fixing?"

Julia shrugged. "I think I'm just going to make stew with some salt pork, and maybe some biscuits to go with it." It was what she cooked when she didn't have much time. Tom never complained, though.

"I'll make the biscuits," Anna offered.

As Julia worked, she kept half an eye on the other woman, immediately feeling inadequate. She had to measure out everything that she put into biscuits while Anna was just taking a handful of one thing and throwing in a little bit of something else. How had she become such a good cook? "Did you cook a lot for your family?"

Anna shook her head. "I was an orphan, raised in the orphanage in Beckham, Massachusetts. I helped in the kitchen there a great deal. When I was too old to stay any longer, I became a teacher, but I really didn't enjoy it, so I decided to become a mail order bride." She looked down at her hands which were covered with flour. "I should have fulfilled my obligations and just come instead of deciding to wait longer."

Julia frowned. "Honestly? I'm glad you waited. I never would have married Tom if you hadn't, and I'm very happy with him." She knew she must sound like she was bragging that she was the one who had married Tom, but she didn't mean to. She was simply happy with her marriage and needed to show it.

Tom opened the door then and stopped short. He walked to Julia and pressed a kiss to her cheek, giving her a confused glance.

"Tom, this is Anna Simmons. I found her standing in the street as the stagecoach drove off. Didn't you send her a telegram?" Julia's eyes met

Tom's as she asked him the question, hoping he would not look at Anna and know she was the perfect woman for him.

Tom shook his head. "I'm so sorry. I plum forgot about it. I should have sent it two weeks ago."

Anna smiled, her eyes not meeting his. "It's all right. I understand that mistakes happen."

Tom frowned. She wouldn't even look at him. She was a pretty girl, but she was nothing compared to his Julia. Julia had flame red hair that made her stand out in a crowd, while Anna's was blond. He'd done much better than the little mousy girl that looked to be afraid of her own shadow. "Where are you going to stay while you're in town?" he asked.

Anna looked at Julia, her eyes begging the other woman to answer for her.

Julia smiled at Anna kindly. "She's going to stay with us until she decides what she's going to do. She's trying to decide if she wants to find a husband here, stay in town to teach, or head back to Massachusetts. I told her if she wants to go home that we'll pay for the ticket." She didn't add that she was going to introduce Anna to the school board on Sunday. He'd see that for himself soon enough, and she didn't want to get his hopes up.

Tom wanted to argue that it wasn't his responsibility to pay for her ticket back to Massachusetts, but he really felt as if it was. He shouldn't have married Julia after she had told him her name, but he had given her no choice. He'd ruined the lives of both women by not listening, but he would do everything he could to make up for it.

Anna sat next to Julia at the table, and she was just as shy as she had stated in her letters. She whispered any time she needed anything. It took about five minutes for Tom to become annoyed. He never would have made it a month without being frustrated with her.

Julia kept up a steady stream of chatter, talking about all her students and how the first two weeks of school had gone. She mentioned that she was more than a little disillusioned with teaching, and Anna nodded.

"That's how I felt after my first year teaching," she whispered. "I really thought I'd have an opportunity to make a difference, but I never did."

Tom eyed Anna. "You were a teacher? You didn't tell me that in your letter."

Anna blushed, obviously hating being the object of his attention. "I'm sure there are a lot of things you don't know about me." She took a bite of her stew, not meeting his eyes.

Tom looked at Julia and frowned. He wondered how long Anna would be staying with them, hoping it wouldn't be long. He wasn't certain how long he could take the constant shyness.

After the meal, Tom sat at the table and watched as the two women worked together. They were obviously becoming friends, and while that was fine with him, it still felt awkward. Of course, Julia knew very few people in the area, so he was pleased she'd found a friend.

Julia sat beside him after finishing the dishes and picked up her crocheting. She was working on a shawl to wear for winter, because she said her coat from the previous year had worn out. She'd hoped not to need a coat in Texas at all, but he'd explained that in the area they were in there were one or two days per year below freezing. It would be much better than being in New York City, though, so she wouldn't complain.

Anna hesitated for a moment, looking between them. Julia smiled at her. "You can stay down here and join us, or you're welcome to go upstairs. I told you where your room is, but there's a bathroom right beside it. With a real porcelain bathtub!" Julia was certain Anna was like her, and had never even seen a real bathtub, let alone used one. She loved the idea of letting her friend use it, as long as she didn't think she should stay there forever and marry her former fiancé.

Anna had given no indication she would even think of doing such a thing, but Julia was more than a little nervous. She was afraid of Tom's feelings for Anna more than anything.

Anna's eyes widened. "Would it be all right if I used it?" she asked.

Julia nodded. "Of course! Make yourself at home here. Please. We're happy to share anything we have." Julia was more than willing to share with the girl, who should have been the mistress of the house, not her. Her feelings were very mixed about Anna. She felt like she should be kind to her and give her everything she owned, because she'd stolen her husband, no matter how inadvertently it had been.

Anna walked toward the stairs, stopping to pick up her bags on the way. She hadn't yet gone up to see her room, because she'd decided to help Julia with dinner instead. Julia and Tom both watched her until she was out of sight before turning to one another.

As soon as she was out of sight, Tom turned to Julia. "How long is she staying here?" he asked.

Julia frowned. She knew he was comparing the two of them, and she was certain she was falling short. Anna was as petite as she was tall, and she had the prettiest blond hair Julia had ever seen. She was the kind of girl who Julia had always felt slightly envious of, and it made her feel uncomfortable. "I'm not certain. She's trying to decide whether she's going to go back to Massachusetts, or try to find someone else looking for a bride here. I'm sure there are plenty of men looking for wives." She watched her husband's face, hoping he wouldn't show any sign of being attracted to the pretty blond.

Tom nodded. "Would you like me to ask around? See if I can find someone she might be interested in marrying?" The sooner he got the woman out of his house and he could go back to being a newlywed, the better, as far as Tom was concerned.

"We'll introduce her around at church on Sunday. She doesn't really have anyone to go home to, so I hope she stays. Besides, I kind of like her. I think the two of us will be good friends." *If she doesn't try to steal my husband from me.* As soon as the thought crossed her mind, Julia felt guilty for it. She was the one who had stolen the other girl's husband, not the other way around. Anna had been very sweet about it as well, not even raising her voice to Julia. She had to be frightened, because she had nowhere to go and knew no one in the state, but she was still pleasant to be around.

Tom sighed. "I'll introduce her to my friends. Maybe one of them was thinking of sending off for a mail order bride." He shook his head. A month ago he'd been excited because he had a bride on the way. Now he had two women living with him, and he really needed to get rid of one of them. The one upstairs, of course. Not his beautiful sweet Julia. How had he ended up in this situation?

Chapter 6

JULIA AND ANNA SPENT the day cleaning the house on Saturday, and they talked while they worked. While Julia scrubbed the floors, Anna washed the breakfast dishes. "I'm sorry that the house was so dirty when you came. I can't seem to keep up with all the cooking, cleaning, and teaching. Something is going to have to give. Maybe that's why teachers aren't allowed to be married. It's just too much work!" She sighed as she thought about all the work that needed to be done, including the entire week's worth of washing. She'd do her baking as well, but she'd have to bake more bread before school a couple of days that week. She hadn't really thought about how she was working two full time jobs until she started doing it.

Anna grinned at her over her shoulder. "You may have a point. I can't imagine even trying to do that much. Why didn't you just resign your position as soon as you married Tom?"

Julia thought about the best way to answer that for a minute. "There were a couple of reasons. First of all, I'd agreed to teach for the entire school year, and I believe very strongly in following through on my obligations. Second, teaching has been my parents' dream for me since I was a little girl. They have always worked in factories, and all my friends were leaving school by fourteen to work in the factories there in New York City as well. My parents sacrificed to keep me in school so I could be a teacher. I hate letting them down." And she wouldn't if she could help it. She'd teach for every minute the school board would allow her to teach...whether she liked it or not.

"So, if you didn't want to let them down, why did you marry Tom?"

Julia blushed, not certain what to say to that. Finally, she decided to tell the other woman the truth. "When I first saw Tom walking across the street toward me, all I could think about was how handsome he was, and then when he asked if I was Miss Simmons, and I said I was, he kissed me. My brain turned to mush. I tried to explain everything, but he thought I was you and just being shy, so every time I started to talk about how he had mistaken me for someone else, he'd kiss me again. And my brain would turn to mush again. I finally just went along with it all because I couldn't think straight." She looked off across the room for a moment before she got back to scrubbing the floor. "Tom is a really persuasive kisser." She couldn't believe she'd actually admitted that to the other woman, but it was the truth. His kisses turned her into something she wasn't most of the time, and even after two weeks of marriage it was still the same. He'd kiss her, and her brain would be mush.

Anna stared at Julia in surprise for a moment. "Oh, that would have scared me. I wouldn't have liked it at all. I probably would have gotten back on the stage so fast, he wouldn't have known what happened."

Julie grinned. "It certainly worked on me. I've had boys try to kiss me before, but I always hated it. With Tom? I didn't ever want him to stop." She knew it wasn't the kind of thing she was supposed to talk to an unmarried woman about, but she needed her to understand why she'd married a stranger. It was really an odd thing to have done.

"Oh, I don't think that will ever happen for me." Anna sighed. "I want to marry, but I'm so timid around men. I can see now it never would have worked for Tom and me. He's so...forceful. It would have scared me a great deal."

Julia shook her head. "We'll find you a good man. There are so many more men than women here in Texas. I'm sure you'll have your pick of men who are just perfect for you." She didn't know many men there, yet, but she'd do her research and find just the right one for Anna. She wanted her to stay, but she wanted her to be married, so Tom wouldn't be tempted by her.

"You're kind to say that. I don't know if that's what I want after all, though. Tom seemed so wonderful in his letters, and then I met him, and I'm instantly almost paralyzed with nerves. No, I don't think getting married is the right thing for me right now."

Julia immediately wanted to help her new friend change her mind, but she had no idea how to do it. She didn't want her to leave the area, though, because she was the first friend she'd made since arriving in the state. She said nothing else about it as she finished scrubbing the floors, but her mind was constantly working on how she could get the other woman married off and happy.

JULIA INTRODUCED ANNA around at church the following day. She hadn't met many people yet, but she at least knew Mr. Hanson, the head of the school board. He was the man Julia had agreed to board with during her year there, and he very obviously loved the idea of hiring Anna in Julia's place. Julia wanted to poke the man in the eye with a rusty fork for his antiquated ways, but she was glad he took an interest in her friend.

"So you've taught before? What's your experience?" he asked, obviously deciding to interview her right there and just get the whole thing over with.

Anna clutched Julia's hand to give her courage, obviously very nervous under the steely gaze of Mr. Hanson. "I taught for two years at a small rural school outside of Beckham, Massachusetts. I boarded with a local family while I taught there."

Mr. Hanson nodded. "My wife and I have agreed to board the new teacher, whomever she may be. Our children are out of the house now, but I'm on the school board, and we live just across the street from the schoolhouse."

"That sounds as if it would work for me." Anna dug into the draw string purse she had attached to her wrist. "I brought my teaching credentials in case you needed to see them."

Mr. Hanson looked over the paper. "This seems to be in order. Yes, absolutely. I'll talk to the others, but I believe we'll be offering you a job. Where are you staying?"

"I'm staying with Julia and Tom Harding. I was supposed to marry Tom," Anna said softly.

Mr. Hanson glared at Julia. "Yes, I've heard what happened there. It's why I'm looking for a new teacher." He shook his head. "I hope your morals are stronger than the last teacher we hired. We will offer you forty dollars a month for teaching, minus ten dollars a month for room and board. Would that be acceptable should we offer you the position?"

Anna nodded. "That sounds more than fair."

Julia shook her head as Mr. Hanson walked off to go speak with the other members of the school board. "He makes me so angry! It's like he doesn't have the ability to remember what it's like to meet someone and be attracted to them." She muttered under her breath, angrier than she could ever remember being. How dare he be so bigoted about her? He simply had no right!

Anna smiled. "Don't listen to him. He's just trying to do his job, even if he's going about it in a very odd way."

Julia sighed. "Oh, I know. I'm working hard to make certain the children are taught well, even though he makes me angry. I'm honestly looking forward to the day when I can be a full-time wife. Teaching here is not what I imagined teaching would be." She didn't mind the teaching, but she wished there was a way to help the children more than she did. She honestly felt like she was wasting her time when most of them could simply do the work in their books without her.

Anna patted Julia's arm. "Nothing is ever exactly what you think it will be. I had Tom all built up in my head to be an almost god-like man. I get here, and he's just like every other man I've ever met."

Julia laughed. "I had never heard of him, but I think he's pretty wonderful. I guess it's all in the eye of the beholder, isn't it?" She couldn't imagine a woman seeing Tom for the first time and not simply falling at his feet. He'd had her stomach filled with butterflies before they even met.

Mr. Hanson came back then, interrupting their giggles. "The school board has voted to offer you the position. You may start tomorrow."

"Tomorrow? That soon? But..."

"Is there a problem with that, Miss Simmons?" Mr. Hanson raised an eyebrow as if just waiting for her to argue with him.

"No, sir." Anna looked at Julia, her eyes full of anxiousness.

Julia smiled sweetly. "We'll get you packed and take you to Mr. Hanson's house this evening, Anna. It's no problem." At least she hoped it wasn't. Tom may have other plans, but he usually kept his Sundays open. It was their only day they spent together every week. Now that she was teaching, their time seemed to be very scarce.

"I should think not. It's going to be hard enough for those children to have to switch teachers mid-term. We'll make the transition as smooth as possible." He looked at Julia. "You'll be paid for the half month you worked. Good day." He turned on his heel and left them standing there.

Anna's eyes were wide, as if she didn't quite comprehend what had just happened.

Julia shook her head. "Oh, that man! He angers me more than just about anyone I've ever met. I'm thrilled I won't be working for him any longer." She sighed. "Let's go tell Tom." She watched Anna's face as she made the suggestion, knowing the other woman was intimidated by her husband. She just wished she wasn't so worried about Tom's feelings about Anna. She did know without a doubt that if Tom had feelings for Anna, they were not reciprocated.

Anna wrinkled her nose. "Do we have to?"

Julia laughed softly, looping her arm through Anna's. "We do need to be certain Tom doesn't have any more plans for the evening so we can get him to bring us into town. I'm glad we did the laundry yesterday, so you won't have to worry about it for a bit while you're living with the

Hanson's." She didn't want to think about what life would be like living under the Hanson's roof. She did not envy her friend one bit.

Anna was obviously thinking along the same lines. "I can't imagine what life is going to be like living in that man's house."

"Well, he has nothing against you, because you're rescuing him. He's angry with me for being a loose woman and marrying." Julia grinned slightly, leaning over to whisper in Anna's ear. "I wonder if he tells his wife she's a loose woman for marrying him." She knew she was out of line for even suggesting such a thing, but she couldn't help herself.

Anna clapped her hand over her mouth to keep from giggling. "Now when I meet the woman, that's all I'm going to think about. What are you doing to me?"

Julia giggled. "Everyone needs a friend who will be a bad influence on them. I guess that's who I'll be for you." They reached Tom, and he looked at their linked arms and grinned.

"You two look like you're having a good time. Have you been introducing Anna around?" He couldn't help but hope that Anna had met the man of her dreams and would be walking with him to the pastor to ask him to marry them immediately. He knew it wasn't at all possible, but he still smiled at the idea.

Julia knew immediately that he was asking if she'd introduced the other girl to any prospective husbands. "In a way. I introduced her to Mr. Hanson, and she's taking over for me as teacher starting tomorrow. Do you mind driving her into town this evening so she can move to Mr. Hanson's, where she'll live for the rest of the school year?" She knew Tom wouldn't mind, but she wasn't willing to take him for granted. He was a good husband to her, and she needed to be certain to always treat him with respect.

Tom shook his head. "I don't mind at all." He hoped his face didn't show how excited he was at the prospect. He was ready to get rid of the girl. She wasn't at all how he'd pictured her.

Julia smiled. "That settles it then. We'll all drive in together this evening." She knew that Anna wouldn't want to be alone with Tom for the drive into town. She was too nervous around him. She immediately started thinking about what she'd fix for supper to make it easier on the others.

When Anna came down the stairs after supper that evening carrying her carpet bags, she hugged Julia tightly. "I've never had a friend like you. I'm so glad I'm staying in the area so we can get to know one another better."

"I feel the same way. I've spent my whole life studying all the time so that I could become a good teacher. I've never really had time to make friends. I'm so glad we've gotten to know each other and that we can be friends. Our circumstances are...odd." She knew that was an understatement, but she wasn't certain how else to say it. The other woman had been wonderful to her, and she was certain she wouldn't have been as sweet tempered and forgiving if the situation had been reversed.

Anna laughed. "That's putting it mildly. I never thought I would meet the woman who married my fiancé and actually like her!"

Tom came into the house then and picked up Anna's bags. "Is this all you brought?" he asked. It was the same amount that Julia had come with, but for some reason, he was surprised Anna had brought so little. He saw Anna as someone who was much more vain about her appearance than Julia, although he'd seen nothing that would make him feel that way.

Anna nodded, her face suddenly shy and serious. "Yes."

Tom turned away so she wouldn't see the exasperation on his face. If he'd married her, he would have strangled her within a week. She just made him crazy. He hoped she had a good life, though, as long as it wasn't as his bride.

On the way into town, Julia sat between Tom and Anna on the buckboard, talking nonstop about the area and what she'd discovered so far. "There's a town near here that's said to have healing waters. People drink them and bathe in them from what I understand. It's called Mineral Wells." When Anna didn't really respond, she continued. "Weatherford seems to be a real hub of activity around here. Did you take the train into Weatherford like I did?" she asked. Julia couldn't help but wish one of the other two would say something, anything, to contribute to the conversation, but while they both talked to her constantly, they seemed to have nothing to say to one another.

The Hanson's house was big, and they were obviously people of wealth. When Tom pulled up, Anna frowned around Julia, who sat between her and Tom. "Are you certain this is the right place? It's so big." The look on her face made it plain she was intimidated by the huge house.

Tom nodded. "Yes, Mr. Hanson is the richest man in town." He got down and helped Anna down and got her bags from the back. He looked at Julia. "Are you getting down?" He knew she wasn't fond of Mr. Hanson, but he wanted to at least make certain she knew she could come if she wanted to.

Julia shook her head. "I'm not going anywhere near that judgmental man." She folded her arms across her chest and looked out over the street, waiting for the others to return. She'd wait in the wagon for three hours rather than go with them into Mr. Hanson's house.

Tom was startled to hear Anna's indrawn breath, and he looked at her worriedly. He was surprised to see that she was laughing with her hand covering her mouth to keep from guffawing in the street. "You find Julia's attitude toward Mr. Hanson amusing?" he asked. It was the most emotion he'd seen from the woman, and he was astonished that she was that amused over his wife's utter disgust with the head of the school board.

She simply nodded, not meeting his eyes. She turned to walk up the stone walkway to the front door and knocked. An older woman, probably in her mid-fifties, with gray hair and tired-looking blue eyes, answered the door. "I'm Anna Simmons."

The door was opened wide. "I'm Dorothy Hanson. Welcome." She eyed Tom. "Just give Miss Simmons her bags. While a single lady is living in this house, there will be no men allowed."

Tom nodded and set the bags down, turning back to the wagon. He wasn't going to argue with the old biddy. He was too happy to be going home with his wife, where there were no guests, and where she wouldn't have to rush to get ready for bed because she had to teach in the morning. He climbed onto the seat beside Julia and wrapped his arm around her shoulders. "I'm glad that it's going to be just us again." His bite on her ear left her in no doubt about what he was planning for their evening alone together.

Julia nodded. "I am too. I'm really glad Anna accepted the position. I hope she enjoys it more than I did. Working for Mr. Hanson made me just a little bit crazy." She'd never met anyone like the man, and she honestly hoped she never did again. She would have liked to ask Tom to switch churches, but she knew that she could avoid Mr. Hanson if she needed to, and she wanted to see Anna regularly.

"Both of the Hansons are judgmental bigots. I almost feel sorry for Anna having to live with them. Of course, I don't feel sorry enough for her to ask her to live with us." They'd reached the edge of town, and he leaned down and nipped at her neck. "I'm too happy with my new wife to care too much about her." He wanted to pull her into the wagon bed with him right there and then, but he knew she would protest. He'd have to wait until they arrived home, and he could. Just barely.

Julia sighed contentedly, leaning against him. "I was really worried that when you saw her, you were going to realize that you'd made a mistake by marrying me and want her instead." She hadn't spoken the words aloud to him before that, choosing instead to worry in silence. Now that the other woman was gone, she felt free to express her worries.

Tom laughed. "She's afraid of her own shadow. She would have driven me crazy in less than a week. I need a fiery redhead who's not afraid to speak her mind and call her employer judgmental." He couldn't have found a woman more perfect for him even if he'd known what he was looking for to ask for it specifically.

"Well, that's certainly what you've got with me." She said nothing else as they drove home, content that he didn't want Anna once and for all. She certainly wanted to see her friend find happiness, but she knew she could survive for the rest of the school year with the Hansons. She'd keep her eyes peeled and find the best possible husband for Anna, even though Anna didn't feel like she could marry. She needed to find a man who was just as shy as Anna was. It may not be an easy job, but she knew she could do it.

Chapter 7

THEY'D BEEN MARRIED about a month when Julia received a letter from her parents. She waited until Tom went back to work after unloading their purchases from their trip into town before she sat down to read it. She was very nervous about what they'd have to say. She hoped they wouldn't judge her too harshly.

"Dear Julia, We're thrilled to hear about your marriage to Tom. He sounds like a really good man. I think you misunderstood our intentions all along. We wanted you to teach, but only so you would have a way out of New York and not be forced to spend your life working in factories as we have. We both wish you the best, knowing that you'll be happy and not forced to come back here again. Hopefully we'll be able to make a trip out to see you someday, but even if we don't, please know that you have all our love. Please write. I'm ready to hear that I have a grandchild on the way. All our love, Mama and Papa."

Julia let out a breath, feeling tension she didn't know she'd been holding inside leave her body. She'd been so worried her parents would be angry with her about her decision to marry, and not teach, that she'd been almost afraid to write to them and tell them what she'd done.

She carefully folded the letter and put it into the pocket of her apron and started supper, knowing she would cook a good celebratory meal that evening. Tom had just sold several of his cattle, and they had some extra money, so she'd splurged a bit on fabrics to make some cushions for the chairs and curtains. She wanted to make her house a special home.

When Tom came in for supper, she served the meal and sat down across from him, bowing her head automatically for his prayer. As he was putting the food onto his plate, he asked, "What did you mother have to say?" He was surprised she hadn't already offered the information.

Julia was astonished to feel tears sting her eyes as she answered. "She's thrilled that I'm married. It wasn't so much that she wanted me to teach as that she wanted me to get out of New York and not spending the rest of my life working in a factory like she did." She sighed happily. "They're being so much more positive about it than I thought they would be." The excitement she felt at having their blessing showed clearly on her face.

Tom smiled, loving how happy she was. "Does that mean you feel better about everything, and you're not worried anymore?" he asked.

She nodded. "It does. I'm sorry it's been on my mind so much, but I couldn't help but worry. I mean, I'm thrilled to have you as a husband, and I'm very happy, but it was always in the back of my mind that my parents would be angry when they found out. Knowing they're pleased has made the difference for me."

"Well, I hope you know, I don't care if they're happy or not...I'm not letting you go. I love you too much to give you up now." He said the words nonchalantly as if he told her he loved her every day.

She stared at him in surprise for a moment. "You love me? You didn't just settle for me because I was the one who got off the stagecoach?" Always in the back of her mind was the thought that if Anna had gotten off the stage, he would have taken one look at her and wanted to stay with her forever. She was glad it had been her, but she couldn't feel like it should have been.

He chuckled. "Of course, I didn't. You can't believe that." Didn't he show her in little ways every day how much he loved her? Was she blind?

She shook her head. "I was never sure. I mean, I know I love you, but I keep expecting you to realize that Anna was the girl you really wanted. She's so tiny and pretty, and I'm just...me." She felt like she was a giant next to the tiny girl.

"You really didn't need to worry about that. I saw you and knew you were the only woman I would ever want in my life." Even he had been astonished by how quickly he'd fallen for the pretty redhead.

"But you were in love with Anna!" How could his feelings have changed so quickly? Would they change again?

Tom frowned. "I sent two letters to her, and she received one from me. That's the only communication we ever had with one another. I wasn't in love with her. I was excited about having a bride, but you ended up being that bride for me, not her." He shuddered to think what life would have been like if he'd married Anna and not Julia. He may have grown to be content, but he never would have been truly happy like he was with Julia.

"Really? I thought you'd been writing longer, I guess. It never occurred to me that she was as much of a stranger to you as I was." She looked down at her hands, worried for a moment. "You really don't mind that you married me and not her?" Despite his words, she had to ask one more time to be certain.

He shook his head adamantly. "Of course, I don't mind. I saw you and fell in love. I saw her and was annoyed almost instantly by the way she wouldn't meet my eyes. She said she was shy, and I thought I could handle that, but she'd have driven me crazy." He wasn't exactly certain why she annoyed him so much, but she was the absolute opposite of Julia in so many ways. It wouldn't have worked out between them, and he knew it.

Julia frowned. "I guess that just goes to show you how differently men and women see things. I saw her and thought that she would be any man's ideal woman. She's tiny, pretty, and soft spoken." She must be crazy listing the other woman's good qualities, but she had to make certain he realized that she was good wife material.

He laughed. "She's so short I would get a crick in my neck when I kissed her. I prefer your looks. Your hair looks like it's about to catch fire to me, and I think that's beautiful. And she's so soft spoken that I can't hear anything she says. She won't look at me when she talks, and that's very annoying." He spoke of the things that had made him realize that she wasn't the woman for him, while making certain that each thing made Julia feel more beautiful.

Julia just shook her head. "We need to find her a good man to marry. One who won't mind her shyness." She was positively excited at the idea of finding a good husband for her friend.

Tom rolled his eyes at her, laughing. "Are you going to start playing match maker?"

Julia shrugged. "I just might. I like the idea of providing her with a husband since I feel like I stole hers." She was, and always would be, full of remorse for her part in ruining Anna's life.

Tom walked around the table and took her hand, pulling her to her feet. "You didn't you know. I'd have married her, but I never would have belonged to her heart and soul like I belong to you. I love you, Julia. You were the woman God created just for me, and I can't imagine spending my life with anyone else." What more could he say to make her realize she was perfect in his eyes?

Julia sighed, resting her head on his shoulder. "I never thought I'd feel this way about anyone." She kissed his chin. "I'm glad you were the one to pick me up from the stagecoach. I wouldn't change a moment of our lives together."

Tom closed his eyes and rested his cheek atop her head. "I wouldn't either. I'm so glad you said that. I've been feeling guilty about forcing you into marriage from the moment I realized that you weren't the woman I thought you were. I never wanted to go back and marry Anna, but I felt guilty for being so determined to keep you."

Julia grinned. "No more guilt is necessary. I love you, and I am so glad we got married." She looked down at the dishes on the table for a moment and decided to ignore them. Instead, she pulled him toward the bedroom and shut the door, shutting out the whole world. She was right where she needed to be, in the arms of the man she loved.

Epilogue

ANNA SAT ON HER BED in the Hansons' house and wrote a quick letter to Elizabeth Miller, the owner of the mail order bride agency who had placed her with Tom. "Dear Elizabeth, You asked me to write to you when I was married and settled to let you know I was all right. I'm not married, but I do appear to be settled. When I arrived, two weeks late as you know, Tom had 'accidentally' married another woman. I can't make myself be angry, because you look at the two of them, and you can see the love that radiates off them both as they look at one another. Tom seemed so sweet in his letters, but...I can't see myself married to him. We really don't belong together. I'm not certain what I'm going to do from here, but I have no desire to try to be a mail order bride again at this time. I'm going to teach at least until the end of the school year and see what happens from there. According to Julia, the woman I should hate but find I'm extremely fond of, there are a great deal of unmarried men around here just looking for wives. I may teach for a year and then look for a husband, or I may just continue teaching. I don't know. But I'm here and settled for now, so you no longer need to worry about me. If I decide to be a mail order bride again, I will write to you and let you know. I honestly don't see that happening though. My life would have been miserable married to Tom. Thank you for all the help you gave me. I'm glad to be out of Beckham, and I've made a very good friend. She's probably the best friend I've ever had. She's here and has promised to do her best to look out for me. I will continue to write if you wish it, but please don't worry. Sincerely, Anna."

She folded the letter to mail on her way to school the following morning. After three weeks of teaching at the Wiggieville school, she knew exactly what to expect, all except for the new boy, of course. He'd been in town for less than a week, and he was a trouble maker like she'd never seen. His mother had died somewhere back east, so she'd sent a letter to his father to come see her at the school. She was not looking forward to meeting the man and talking to him about his son's behavioral issues. The boy was a hellion, and she didn't know what else she was going to be able to say about him.

AS SOON AS SCHOOL WAS dismissed Monday afternoon, Anna stood to wipe the blackboard clean and write out the assignments for Tuesday. She was exhausted. Ernie Hoover, her new student, had caused as much havoc in the school as he possibly could. He'd come in late, blocked the outhouse door with one of the other young boys inside, refused to study, and basically just mad her day as difficult as he could.

She heard footsteps behind her and she turned around, looking to see who was there. A man of medium height and build, with dark hair and brown eyes the color of chocolate, stood at the back of the school with his hand clamped firmly on Ernie's shoulder. So this was his father.

She walked toward the back of the room, swallowing hard, because she always had a hard time talking to men, and she was certain this man would be no exception. Once she reached the back of the room, she looked down at Ernie who was squirming under his father's hand. "Go on out to the schoolyard, Ernie. I need to speak with your father privately."

Ernie looked at his father, and stuck his tongue out at Anna before running from the room. Anna waited for Mr. Hoover to say something to correct the boy, but when he didn't she all but growled. "Do you always let him get away with disrespectful behavior, Mr. Hoover?"

Mr. Hoover raised an eyebrow before sticking this thumbs through the belt loops of his work pants and looking her up and down. "Do you always let your students treat you disrespectfully and expect their parents to fix the problem? I assure you, Miss Simmons, I don't have time to sit in your classroom all day and do *your* job."

Anna saw red. She'd never been so angry at a man in her entire life. Normally, she would be afraid to react to the criticism, but she was furious. She took a step toward him, her tiny stature still having to look way up to him despite him not being taller than average. "If you were doing *your* job and raising the boy right in the first place, he wouldn't dare to think of being disrespectful in my classroom!"

"Who do you think you are telling me I'm not raising my boy right?" He took one more step forward, and the two of them were all but brushing their bodies up against one another as they faced each other.

"Are you telling me that you don't think you should have to teach your boy to behave correctly in the first place and it's my job to both parent *and* teach him?" As soon as the words were out of her mouth, she knew she'd gone too far, but she couldn't take them back. She bit her lip, waiting to see what the man would say or do.

Jesse Hoover's eyes flashed as he stared down at the tiny little spitfire of a teacher. He knew Ernie was trouble. He had been ever since his mother had died, but it wasn't Jesse's job to deal with him while Ernie was at school. He was only eight. What kind of teacher couldn't deal with an eight year old boy? "Don't you have a ruler you can use on his knuckles?"

Anna's eyes grew even wider. "If he was disciplined properly at home, I wouldn't have to resort to corporal punishment in my classroom. If I have to get the ruler out, then I will have to disrupt the entire class to use it. If you will just discipline him at home and make it clear that you will back up whatever I say, then we won't have any more issues!"

Jesse was so angry he wanted to hit the woman. He stared down into her pretty face and realized hitting her wasn't what he wanted to do. He wanted to kiss her. He grabbed her by the waist and pulled her to him, his mouth crushing hers with a hard kiss, his tongue immediately demanding entrance.

Anna stood paralyzed for a moment, not believing this man was actually touching her. Didn't he know she was his son's teacher? It only took a moment for her to feel her stomach fill with longing. She put her hands up to his shoulders to push him away, and instead, she grasped them and clung to him. Her mind was no longer functioning. What was he doing to her?

After a moment, Jesse lifted his head, staring down at the pretty little teacher. Her hair was coming down from the sides of her bun, where it had been pinned up severely. Her lips, a bright pink and moist from his kiss, were still parted, and she was panting slightly. She was a teacher? She looked like she should be a dancer in the local saloon. Not her clothes, of course, but the wanton look on her face. He stared at her for a moment, waiting for her to open her eyes and realize exactly what she was doing.

Anna blinked a few times, returning to reality. Instead of agreeing to discipline his child properly, he had kissed her instead. She had never been kissed before, and the first time she was, it was by a man whose first name she didn't even know. What was wrong with her?

She took a step back, just as she saw the pink fabric of the skirt of a dress disappear around the corner. "Oh blast! Someone just saw that. I'm going to lose my job!" She folded her arms across her chest for a moment, glaring at him.

Jesse's eyes widened. Her stance was all but demanding to know what he was going to do about her impending job loss. "I guess you shouldn't be going around kissing your students' fathers instead of working then, should you?"

Anna clenched her fists, not believing this man would really say that to her. "I trust that you'll talk to Ernie and get his behavior under control so that I don't have to expel him. Good day, Mr. Hoover." She turned and walked regally to her desk on the raised platform at the front of the room, and sank into her chair.

She watched as he stared at her for a moment before shaking his head, and walking from the room. She was a little snob, and he wasn't going to deal with her any longer. His son was fine. He was just a boy. That woman was just going to have to learn how to deal with boys.

Once in the schoolyard, he grabbed Ernie's hand and started toward home. Just as he left the schoolyard, he heard himself say, "When we get home, I'm going to take a belt to your bottom like I should have done years ago, boy. You will not show that kind of disrespect to anyone, but most especially your teacher."

He had no clue where the words had come from, but once they were out, he almost smiled. Yes, Ernie needed to be taken in hand. He'd never tell that little spitfire of a teacher he agreed with her, though. No way.